Y0-BPT-954

A NOTE TO PARENTS

When your children are ready to "step into reading," giving them the right books—and lots of them—is as crucial as giving them the right food to eat. **Step into Reading Books** present exciting stories or information reinforced with lively, colorful illustrations that make learning to read fun, satisfying, and worthwhile. They are priced so that acquiring an entire library of them is affordable. And they are beginning readers with an important difference—they're written on three levels.

Step 1 Books, with their very large type and extremely simple vocabulary, have been created for the very youngest readers. **Step 2 Books** are both longer and slightly more difficult. **Step 3 Books,** written to mid-second-grade reading levels, are for the child who has acquired even greater reading skills.

Children develop at different ages. **Step into Reading Books,** with their three levels of reading, are designed to help children become good—and interested—readers *faster*. The grade levels assigned to the three steps—preschool through grade 1 for Step 1, grades 1 through 3 for Step 2, and grades 2 and 3 for Step 3—are intended only as guides. Some children move through all three steps very rapidly; others climb the steps over a period of several years. These books will help your child "step into reading" in style!

Library of Congress Cataloging in Publication Data:

Rosenbloom, Joseph. Deputy Dan gets his man. (Step into reading. A Step 3 book) SUMMARY:
Deputy Dan sets out to foil Shootin' Sam's dastardly plan to rob a train.   1. Children's stories,
American.   [1. Robbers and outlaws—Fiction.   2. West (U.S.)—Fiction.   3. Humorous stories]
I. Raglin, Tim, ill.   II. Title.   III. Series: Step into reading.   Step 3 book.
PZ7.R719176Dg   1985   [E]   85-1686   ISBN: 0-394-87250-9 (trade); 0-394-97250-3 (lib. bdg.)

Manufactured in the United States of America   1 2 3 4 5 6 7 8 9 0

STEP INTO READING is a trademark of Random House, Inc.

Step into Reading

Deputy Dan

GETS HIS MAN

by Joseph Rosenbloom

illustrated by Tim Raglin

A Step 3 Book

Random House 🏠 New York

Text copyright © 1985 by Joseph Rosenbloom. Illustrations copyright © 1985 by Tim Raglin.
All rights reserved under International and Pan-American Copyright Conventions. Published
in the United States by Random House, Inc., New York, and simultaneously in Canada by
Random House of Canada Limited, Toronto.

My name is Deputy Dan.

I live in Gulch City.

Gulch City is a peaceful place.
My job is to keep it that way.

It is Tuesday, December second.
It is cold.

I am in Sheriff Digbee's office.
Sheriff Digbee is my boss.

"I feel like a cup of tea," says Sheriff Digbee.

"That's funny," I reply. "You don't look like one."

"I meant a cup of tea would be nice," Sheriff Digbee tells me. "Please put the kettle on."

I always follow orders.

"You want me to put the kettle on? Right away, boss!"

I balance the kettle on my head.

Sheriff Digbee sees the kettle. "Why is the kettle on your head?" he asks.

"You told me to put the kettle on. I was just following orders."

"No, NO!" says Sheriff Digbee. "I meant to put the kettle on the stove. Never mind, I'll take care of the tea. Here are some letters. Please stamp them."

"You want me to stamp the letters? Sure thing, boss!"

I spread the letters on the floor. I stamp on the letters over and over again.

When Sheriff Digbee returns with the tea, he is puzzled. "What are you doing?" he asks.

"You told me to stamp the letters. I'm stamping on them as hard as I can, boss."

"No, NO!" says Sheriff Digbee. "When I asked you to stamp the letters, I did not mean to stamp on them with your feet! I meant to put postage stamps on them."

Suddenly there is a knock.

The door bursts open.

Mortimer Q. Fenton rushes in.
He owns the railroad.

"The train has been robbed!" he gasps.

"What was stolen?" Sheriff Digbee asks.

"Mrs. Snodgrass's pearls!" cries
Mortimer Q. Fenton.

Sheriff Digbee turns to me.
"Deputy Dan, I am putting you in charge.
Find the robbers!"

"Will do, boss!" I say.

2

I decide to visit Mrs. Snodgrass.

Mrs. Snodgrass is rich. She lives in the biggest house in Gulch City.

A butler opens the door. He looks me up and down.

"Yes?" he says.

"Is Mrs. Snodgrass home?" I ask.

"Who is calling?"

"I am not calling," I tell him.
"I am speaking in a regular voice."

"I meant who are you?"

"Deputy Dan," I reply.

"This way, please," says the butler.
He leads me to Mrs. Snodgrass.

She has been crying. Her eyes are red.

A little white dog with a big pink
bow sits on her lap.

The little dog growls at me.

"Now, now, Fifi, dear," Mrs. Snodgrass
says to the dog. "Deputy Dan is a
nice man.

"Won't you join me in a cup of hot
chocolate?" she asks me.

"Thanks," I say. "But I don't think
there will be room for both of us
in one little cup."

"I meant would you care for some hot chocolate?"

"Yes, please," I say.

The butler goes to fetch it.

Mrs. Snodgrass's eyes fill with tears. "Deputy Dan," she sobs, "you must catch the robber!"

"I will try."

"That awful man not only stole my pearls, he was rude! And he was mean to my darling Fifi!"

"What happened?" I ask.

"I was riding on the train," says Mrs. Snodgrass. "A man sat down next to me. He kept staring at my pearls. He had no manners at all!

"Fifi did not like him either. She
attacked his shoe and would not let go.

"The man said that if Fifi did not
stop, he would eat her on a roll—
with mustard!

"Can you imagine anyone saying
such a cruel thing?" Mrs. Snodgrass
kisses Fifi.

"What happened then?" I ask.

"He kicked my darling Fifi! Then he grabbed my pearls and jumped off the train."

"What did he look like?"

"He was big and tall. He had a long black moustache and a patch over his left eye."

"That can only be one man," I say. "Shootin' Sam."

"Who is Shootin' Sam?"

"He is the meanest man in the West."

"How true!" sobs Mrs. Snodgrass.

3

It is Wednesday, December third. It is cloudy.

I am sitting in the sheriff's office. Mortimer Q. Fenton comes in.

"Did you find out who stole the pearls?" he asks.

"Yes," I reply. "It was Shootin' Sam."

Mortimer Q. Fenton shudders.

"Not Shootin' Sam, the meanest man in the West?" he asks.

I nod.

Mortimer Q. Fenton looks worried.

"A shipment of gold nuggets will be on the train tomorrow," he says. "What if Shootin' Sam tries to steal it?"

"Deputy Dan, I want you to protect that gold shipment," Sheriff Digbee tells me. "Board the train tomorrow!"

"Will do, boss!"

I start to think. How can I board
a train? I think of one way to do it.
I think of another way. Then I think of
a third way. All the ways take a lot
of wood.

"One question, boss," I say. "Where
do I get the wood to board the train?"

"No, NO!" Sheriff Digbee tells me.
"When I asked you to board the train,
I did not mean to cover the train
with wood. I meant to get on the train!"

"I hear you, boss!"

"And remember," says Sheriff Digbee,
"be on your watch at all times."

"Boss!" I say. "If I am on my watch,
it will break!"

Sheriff Digbee gets very angry. He
grabs his hat. He begins to chew on it.
He chews his hat to pieces. It makes
him feel better.

"When I asked you to be on your
watch," he says, "I did not mean you
should stand on your watch. I meant
you should keep your eyes and ears open."

"Got it, boss!"

4

It is Thursday, December fourth.
It is foggy.

I am carrying two bags. One bag
is marked "Gold Nuggets." The other
is marked "Worthless Pebbles."

I get on the train.

I put the two bags under my seat.

The train starts.

Ten miles out of town the train stops.

The biggest, meanest, toughest, roughest man I ever saw jumps on the train. He has a big black moustache. He wears a patch over his left eye. It is Shootin' Sam!

"I hear there is a shipment of gold on this train," he growls. "Who has it?"

He pulls out his gun.

"Help! Save us!" cry the people on the train.

"Calm down, everyone!" I say. "I will handle this."

I go up to Shootin' Sam. I flash my badge.

"I am Deputy Dan!" I tell him.

He points his gun at me.

I am not afraid.

"You are under arrest!" I say.

"Do you know who you are talking to?" he asks.

"Of course I know who I am talking to. You are Shootin' Sam. They say you are the meanest man in the West."

"That's right!" he says. "I am so mean, I scare ghosts. I am so tough, I eat beans without opening the can. I am so strong, I fight bears with both hands tied behind my back. So don't you try to stop me. I am going to hold up this train!"

I laugh. "You may be strong. But no one is strong enough to hold up a train."

"I did not mean I would lift up the train. I meant I would stick up the train."

"It takes a lot of glue to stick up a train," I say. "Where will you—"

But Shootin' Sam does not let me finish.

"Shut up!" he snarls. "Hand over the money—or else!"

"There are two bags under my seat," I say. "Take your pick."

He looks at the two bags.

"I'll take the one marked 'Gold Nuggets,'" he tells me.

"Are you sure you want that bag?"

"Of course I'm sure!"

I shrug. "Have it your way."

Shootin' Sam grabs the bag marked "Gold Nuggets."

He jumps off the train.

He rides away on his horse.

5

Ten minutes later the train stops.

Shootin' Sam is back.

He is mad.

"You tricked me!" he growls.
"The bag you gave me was filled with
worthless pebbles."

"I did not give you the bag. You
took it. Remember?"

"Well, the other bag under your seat must be the one I want. Only this time I am going to make sure. Open the bag!"

I take the bag from under my seat. It is marked "Worthless Pebbles."

I am about to open the bag, when I see a bug on it.

Shootin' Sam sees it too. He turns white. He groans. His knees knock together.

"What's wrong?" I ask.

"I am not afraid of grizzly bears, or wildcats, or rattlesnakes," says Shootin' Sam. "But bugs are something else. I hate them!"

"I must remember that," I tell myself. I open the bag.

It is filled with gold nuggets. Shootin' Sam grabs the bag.

"I am rich!" he shouts. "Rich!"

"You won't get away with this,"
I warn.

Shootin' Sam glares at me. "You talk
too much, Deputy Dan. I am tired of
listening to you. In fact, I am going
to shoot you."

"Wait!" I say. "A person who is
about to die is allowed one last request."

"True," says Shootin' Sam. "What is
your last request?"

"I want to ask you a riddle."

"All right. But only one."

"What is furry, brown and yellow,
has wings, big green eyes, twenty legs,
and a long stinger on its tail?"

"Sounds horrible," says Shootin' Sam.
"What is it?"

"I don't know. But it's crawling up
your back!"

"Eek!" screams Shootin' Sam. "Help! Get it off me! Quick!"

Shootin' Sam is so scared, he drops his gun.

He does not see me pull out my handcuffs. Before he knows it, he is my prisoner.

I search Shootin' Sam. I find Mrs. Snodgrass's pearls in his pocket.

"This reminds me of another riddle," I say. "What is the longest sentence in the world?"

"I don't know," replies Shootin' Sam. "What?"

"The one the judge is going to give you. It will take you fifty years to finish it."

It is Friday, December fifth. It is
sunny.

I am sitting in the sheriff's office.

Sheriff Digbee and I are having
brownies and milk.

Mortimer Q. Fenton and
Mrs. Snodgrass come in. Mrs. Snodgrass
is carrying Fifi in her arms.

"Thank you for saving the gold," says Mortimer Q. Fenton.

"And thank you so much, Deputy Dan, for getting my precious pearls back," says Mrs. Snodgrass.

Even Fifi seems glad to see me. She does not even growl when I pat her head.

Mortimer Q. Fenton shakes my hand.
"Please accept this railroad pass as a
reward," he says. "Just show it to the
conductor and you can ride the train for
free. You can hit the road anytime you
like."

"But why should I hit the road?" I ask.
"The road never did anything to me."

Mortimer Q. Fenton laughs. "I did not
mean that you should slap the road.
I meant you should take a trip."

"Thank you," I tell him. "But I
cannot accept a free pass."

"Why not?" asks Sheriff Digbee.

"Because if everyone else has to pay
to ride the train, then so should I."

Then Mrs. Snodgrass speaks up.
"I have a splendid idea," she says.
"There is no statue in Gulch City.
And there ought to be one. Why not
make a statue of Deputy Dan?"

"Yes! Deputy Dan is a real hero,"
says Mortimer Q. Fenton.

"Anyone who captures Shootin' Sam
deserves a statue," says Sheriff Digbee.

Little Fifi wags her tail.

Mrs. Snodgrass smiles.

I smile too. It might be nice to
have a statue of me in Gulch City.

Not many bad people come to town these days. I guess they heard what happened to Shootin' Sam.

Gulch City is peaceful again. And that's the way I, Deputy Dan, like it.